My Weirdest School #10

Miss Newman Isn't Human!

Dan Gutman

Pictures by
Jim Paillot

HARPER
An Imprint of HarperCollinsPublishers

To Alison Gust

My Weirdest School #10: Miss Newman Isn't Human!
Text copyright © 2018 by Dan Gutman
Illustrations copyright © 2018 by Jim Paillot
www.harpercollinschildrens.com

ISBN 978-0-06-242939-1 (pbk. bdg.)–ISBN 978-0-06-242940-7 (library bdg.)

Typography by Laura Mock
17 18 19 20 21   CG/LSCH   10 9 8 7 6 5 4 3 2 1

First Edition

Contents

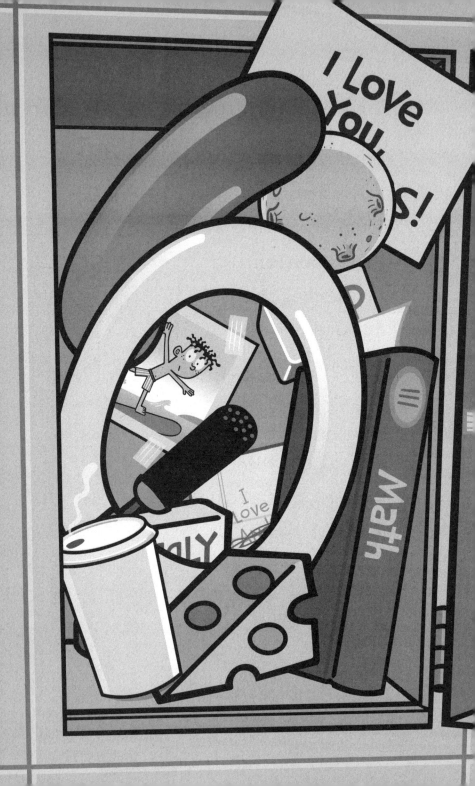

Indoor Recess

My name is A.J. and I hate rain.

Rain is horrible. You can't ride your bike in the rain. You can't play outside. Everything gets soaked. Your sneakers get squishy. You have to wear a dorky raincoat to school.

And then there's the most horrible thing about rain . . .

INDOOR RECESS.

Ugh! Indoor recess was the *worst* invention in the history of the world.*

"I hate rain," I said on Friday morning as I hung up my dorky raincoat in the cloakroom.

"Me too," said my friends Ryan and Michael.

"Me three," said Alexia, this girl who rides a skateboard all the time.

"Me four," said Neil, who we call the nude kid even though he wears clothes.

"But rain is a *good* thing, Arlo," said Andrea Young, this annoying girl with curly brown hair. She calls me by my real

---

*After the solar-powered flashlight.

name because she knows I don't like it. "If we didn't have rain, we wouldn't have water to drink."

"I hate drinking water," I told Andrea.

"If we didn't have rain, we wouldn't have water to fill our bathtubs," Andrea said.

"I hate taking baths."

"The flowers wouldn't grow," Andrea said.

"I hate flowers."

Andrea rolled her eyes.

Her crybaby friend Emily hung up her dorky raincoat next to mine. She was carrying a big plate covered with plastic wrap.

"If we didn't have rain," she said, "we

wouldn't have brownies!"

BROWNIES?!

"I made them with my mom," Emily said. "One of the ingredients is water."

Hmmm. I may have to rethink my position on rain.

That's when our teacher, Mr. Cooper, came flying into the room. And I do mean *flying*. Mr. Cooper thinks he's a superhero. But he's not a very good one. He tripped on an electrical cord and almost knocked over Emily's plate of brownies.

"Good morning!" Mr. Cooper said. "We're going to have a super day!"

"What's your superpower for today, Mr. Cooper?" asked Ryan.

"You've heard of supervision and super-hearing," he said. "Well, I have super*taste*."

Supertaste? I never heard of supertaste.

"Prove that you have supertaste," said Neil.

Mr. Cooper took the plastic wrap off Emily's plate. Then he put a whole brownie in his mouth.

"Mmmm," he said. "This tastes super!"

Mr. Cooper is weird.

Suddenly the voice of our principal, Mr. Klutz, came over the loudspeaker.

"Good morning, Ella Mentry students," Mr. Klutz announced. "I have some good news and some bad news. The good news is that it has stopped raining."

"Yay!" everybody shouted.

"The bad news is, another storm is predicted for this afternoon. So today we will have indoor recess."

Noooooooooo!

Not indoor recess! *Anything* but indoor recess!

I'd rather be chased by wild raccoons than have indoor recess. I'd rather jump off Mount Everest than have indoor recess. I'd rather eat a bowl of *broccoli* than have indoor recess. This was the worst thing to happen since TV Turnoff Week.

"That means we can't play football in the playground," complained Michael.

"No fair!" said Neil.

"I *love* indoor recess," said Andrea, who loves everything I hate. "We can play board games!"

"Board games are fun!" said Emily, who loves everything Andrea loves.

"You mean *bored* games," I said, "because board games are bor-*ring*."

Mr. Klutz wasn't finished with his announcement.

"I have *more* good news, students," he said. "Before the storm arrives this afternoon, I'd like you all to join me on the playground. I have a special surprise."

"Ooooh, I *love* surprises!" said Andrea and Emily, clapping their hands like it was their birthday.

"Okay," shouted Mr. Cooper, "everybody pringle up!"

We all lined up in single file (like Pringles!) and walked a million hundred miles to the playground.

And you'll never believe what happened there.

I'm not going to tell you.

Okay, okay! I'll tell you. But you have to read the next chapter. So nah-nah-nah boo-boo on you!

Sprinkles and Luke Warm

It wasn't raining, but the clouds were dark. It looked like a storm was coming. The whole school was out on the playground.

Well, *actually* it was just the kids and teachers who were out on the playground. It would be weird if the *school* was on the playground.

Mr. Klutz was waiting for us. He has no hair at all. Men lose the hair on their head when they get old, and then it starts growing out of their nose and ears instead. Nobody knows why.

"What's up, Mr. Klutz?" I asked.

"I'll tell you what's up," he replied. He pointed at the sky.

We all looked up. And you'll never believe what we saw.

It was a gigantic hot-air balloon! It was floating down, with a basket under it. On the side of the balloon were the words "CHANNEL 4 WEATHER." It looked like somebody was in the basket.

"Who's that?" Michael asked.

"It looks like Sprinkles Newman, that meteorologist on TV!" shouted Ryan.

"She studies meteors?" I asked. "That's weird."

Everybody laughed even though I didn't say anything funny.

"No, dumbhead," Ryan said. "She's the *weather* lady."

Oh, yeah. My parents watch Sprinkles Newman on Channel 4 every morning before work. She's always talking about the weather. I leave the room when Sprinkles Newman comes on. What a snoozefest. Why do grown-ups care so much about weather? It's just *weather.*

The balloon was hovering over our

heads. Everybody got out of the way so there would be room for it to land. Sprinkles Newman was waving at us.

"Remember when Miss Tracy came to our school and talked about the stars and planets?" Mr. Klutz asked. "Well, that gave me the idea to have Miss Newman come and talk about weather. Wasn't that a great idea?"

"Yes!" shouted all the girls.

"No!" shouted all the boys.

The balloon touched down. Before Miss Newman could climb out of the basket, the weirdest thing in the history of the world happened. A Channel 4 news van came roaring down the street and screeched to a stop at the edge of the playground. A bunch of people jumped out and rushed over to the balloon. One of them started fussing with Miss Newman's hair. Somebody else put makeup on her face. One guy set up lights. Another guy had a video camera.

Finally Miss Newman stepped out of the balloon basket. Everybody clapped and cheered.

A tall guy jumped out of the van and ran over. He was carrying a bunch of big pieces of cardboard. The card on the top of the pile had these words written on it: HI EVERYBODY!

"Hi everybody!" said Miss Newman.

"Hi!" we all shouted.

The tall guy dropped the first piece of cardboard and held up the one underneath it. It said: THANKS FOR INVITING ME TO YOUR SCHOOL.

"Thanks for inviting me to your school," said Miss Newman.

The guy dropped that card and held up the next one. It said: IT'S GREAT TO BE HERE!

"It's great to be here!" Miss Newman said cheerfully.

He held up another card: I LOVE VISITING SCHOOLS AND TALKING WITH KIDS.

"I love visiting schools and talking with

16

kids," said Miss Newman.

He held up another card: I'M SURE WE'LL HAVE A GREAT TIME TODAY!

"I'm sure we'll have a great time today!" said Miss Newman.

The guy kept dropping each card and

holding up the next one for Miss Newman to read.

"Who's that guy?" I asked.

He held up another card: THAT GUY IS MY CUE CARD MAN. HIS NAME IS LUKE. LUKE WARM.

"That guy is my cue card man," said Miss Newman. "His name is Luke. Luke Warm."

How did Luke Warm know I was going to ask who he was? That guy is weird.

That's Gotta Hurt

"Welcome to Ella Mentry School," said Mr. Klutz as he shook Miss Newman's hand. "We're glad to have you here blah blah blah learn about weather blah blah blah enjoy your visit blah blah blah . . ."

He went on like that for a while.

The cue card guy, Luke Warm, held up

a card. It said: THANK YOU VERY MUCH.

"Thank you very much," Miss Newman said.

Luke Warm held up another card: I CAN'T WAIT TO SEE YOUR SCHOOL.

"I can't wait to see your school," said Miss Newman.

"Does Luke Warm have a card for *everything* you say?" asked Alexia.

Luke Warm held up another card. It said: YES, LUKE HAS A CARD FOR EVERYTHING I SAY.

"Yes," said Miss Newman, "Luke has a card for everything I say."

"WOW," we all said, which is "MOM" upside down.

Luke Warm must be really smart to know what people are about to ask. And Miss Newman must be really *dumb* if she has to read everything off cards.

Our reading specialist, Mr. Macky, stepped forward.

"This shows how reading is such an important skill for kids to learn," he said. "No matter what job you have when you grow up, you will probably have to do a lot of reading."

Luke Warm held up another card: OH YES, READING IS VERY IMPORTANT. I LOVE TO READ.

"Oh yes," said Miss Newman. "Reading is very important. I love to read."

Luke Warm was about to hold up another card, but that's when the most amazing thing in the history of the world happened. And we got to see it live and in person.

Suddenly there was a rumbling sound.

The sky got darker.

And then a bright white bolt of lightning came shooting out of the sky!

ZAPPPP!

The lightning bolt hit Luke Warm!

He fell down!

His cue cards scattered everywhere!

Everybody screamed.

"Luke Warm has been struck by lightning!" shouted Andrea.

"Somebody call 911!" shouted Mr. Klutz. "Tell them it's an emergency!"

"Stand back, everyone!" shouted our school nurse, Mrs. Cooney. "Give him some air!"

When Luke Warm hit the ground, Miss Newman shrieked. Then she ran over to where he was lying and held his head in her hands.

That's when the weirdest thing in the history of the world happened. Miss Newman leaned over and started kissing Luke Warm!

"Ooooo!" Ryan said. "Miss Newman is kissing Luke Warm! They must be in *love*!"

"When are they gonna get married?" asked Michael.

"She's not *kissing* him, dumbheads!" shouted Andrea. "She's giving him mouth-to-mouth resuscitation!"

Oh, yeah. Mouth-to-mouth resuscitation is when somebody stops breathing and you blow into their mouth to fill their lungs with air. It looks a lot like kissing, except that one of the kissers happens to be unconscious.

While Miss Newman blew air into Luke Warm's mouth, Mrs. Cooney picked up his hand and held his wrist.

"Is he . . . dead?" asked Michael.

"No, he has a pulse," said Mrs. Cooney.

"But we need to get him to the hospital right away!"

That's when a siren came screaming down the street, and an ambulance pulled up.

"What happened?" yelled one of the paramedics.

"This man was struck by lightning," said Mr. Klutz.

"We'll take care of him," the paramedic replied.

Two paramedics lifted Luke Warm onto a stretcher. They slid it inside the ambulance and drove away with the siren screaming.

Wow, that was scary!

"Okay, everybody pringle up!" Mr. Klutz
shouted. "Let's get inside the gym. Hurry!
We don't want anyone *else* to get hit by
lightning."

Stop Reading This Book!

Wow, pretty exciting, huh?

Wasn't that the most exciting chapter in the history of chapters?

You probably think these books are just silly stories and dumb jokes. But that was serious stuff. Luke Warm was struck by *lightning*! Betcha didn't see *that* coming!

He could have died. Maybe he'll *still*

die! You don't know. Maybe he'll die in the next chapter. That would be really sad.

Ya know what? You should stop reading this book right now. Because it would be *really* upsetting if Luke Warm died. Children's books are supposed to have happy endings where everybody walks off into the sunset together holding hands.

If I were you, I'd ask for my money back from the bookstore. That is, unless you got this book from the library. Then it was free anyway.

Hey, you know how your parents say you have to read a chapter of a book every night? Well, this is the chapter! It counts! You're welcome. And nah-nah-nah boo-boo on your parents.

Atta Girl!

5

Everybody was freaking out in the gym after Luke Warm got struck by lightning. And we saw it with our own eyes.

Well, it would be pretty hard to see something with somebody *else's* eyes.

"He seemed like such a nice man. I hope he'll be okay," said Emily, who always hopes everybody will be okay.

"I'm sure Luke Warm will be fine," said Mr. Klutz.

"Nine out of ten people who get struck by lightning do survive," said Mrs. Cooney.

In the middle of the gym, Miss Newman was just standing there. She wasn't crying. She wasn't saying anything. She looked like she was in shock.

"Are you okay, Miss Newman?" asked Mrs. Cooney.

Miss Newman just stood there, frozen.

"She looks like a deer caught in the headlights," said Mr. Klutz.

What? Miss Newman didn't look *anything* like a deer. She looked like a regular lady. Mr. Klutz needs to get his eyes checked. And I don't think deer get head lice anyway.

Everything Miss Newman had said since she arrived was written on a card for her to read. What was she going to say *now*? I guess everybody was thinking the same thing, because the whole school was looking at her.

Well, not really. Just the kids and teachers were looking at her. Schools don't have eyes.

"I . . . I . . . ," Miss Newman stammered. "I gotta go!" Then she started heading for the door.

"Wait a minute!" Mr. Klutz shouted. "You promised to spend the day talking to our students about the weather. I have a signed contract with Channel 4."

"B-but I . . . I . . . need my cue cards," she replied. "I need Luke."

Then Miss Newman started sobbing and slobbering and blubbering and whimpering and weeping and sniveling. Or some of those things anyway. I'm not sure which ones.

All the lady teachers gathered around

her. Mr. Klutz and all the men teachers stood off to the side of the gym looking uncomfortable.*

"It will be okay, honey," said Ms. Hannah, our art teacher. She gave Miss Newman a hug and a tissue.

"You'll do fine," said Mrs. Roopy, our librarian.

"But . . . I'm *scared*," said Miss Newman.

"You can *do* it, Sprinkles!" said Miss Small, our gym teacher. "Just like you do it on TV every day."

"On TV, Luke tells me what to say," Miss Newman said, wiping her tears away. "I need my cue cards."

---

*Because men have no idea what to do when ladies start crying.

34

"Just be yourself," said Ms. Coco, our gifted and talented teacher. "I bet you've learned a lot doing the weather report on TV all this time."

"That's right," said Miss Holly, our Spanish teacher. "You don't need some *man* telling you what to say."

"Yeah!" shouted all the lady teachers.

Miss Newman stopped crying.

"You know what?" she said. "You're right! It's about time I stood up and spoke for *myself.* I don't need any cue cards!"

"Atta girl!" shouted the lady teachers.

"So," said Mr. Klutz, "would it be okay if the children asked you a few questions about the weather?"

"Sure!" said Miss Newman. "Fire away!"

"Does anybody have a weather question for Miss Newman?" asked Mr. Klutz.

Andrea waved her hand in the air like she was stranded on a desert island trying to signal a plane. Mr. Klutz called on her, as always.

"On TV, you talk a lot about rain," said

Andrea. "What makes it rain?"

Miss Newman thought for a moment.

"Uh . . . ," she said. "It rains because water falls out of the sky. Next question."

WHAT?! That can't be right! I always thought it rained because people in heaven were shooting giant water pistols at us.

Mr. Klutz called on Alexia.

"On TV, you always talk about cold fronts," she said. "Can you tell me what a cold front is?"

"Uh . . . ," said Miss Newman. "A cold front is when the front of something gets cold."

WHAT?! That can't be right! I don't know what a cold front is, but I'm pretty sure it's *not* when the front of something gets cold.

Mr. Klutz called on Michael.

"On TV, you always talk about precipitation," he said. "What *is* precipitation?"

"Uh . . . ," said Miss Newman. "Precipitation is when a person sweats."

WHAT?!

"I think that's *perspiration*," whispered Andrea, the human dictionary.

Lots of kids had hands in the air, but Mr. Klutz stepped up to the front.

"Um, maybe you can tell the children what tonight's weather will be like," he suggested. "You know, give them a forecast of the forecast?"

Miss Newman closed her eyes for a

moment. It was like she was trying to remember her cue cards.

"We can expect an eighty percent chance of weather tonight across the Southwest," she said. "There should be gradual darkness as evening approaches, followed by continued dark through the night, turning partly lighter by morning."

WHAT?! That can't be right!

Miss Newman continued. . . .

"I'm predicting a high pressure blah blah blah increasing blah blah blah temperatures blah blah blah Doppler blah blah blah unseasonable blah blah blah humid air . . ."

She went on like that for a while. I leaned over and whispered in Andrea's ear.

"Is she making any sense at all?" I asked.

"I don't think so," Andrea whispered back. "It sounds like she's just saying random weather words."

"There will be showers across the country tomorrow morning," said Miss Newman, "after people wake up and decide they need to take a shower."

WHAT?! That can't be right!

When Miss Newman finished, the lady teachers gathered around and hugged her. I guess they didn't want to hurt her feelings by telling her she didn't know anything about weather.

"See?" Mrs. Roopy told her. "You did great!"

"You don't need those silly cue cards

after all," said Miss Small.

"Maybe I don't!" Miss Newman said proudly. "Can I tell the children about haboobs now?"

"Haboobs?" everybody asked. "What's a haboob?"

"A haboob is a sandstorm," said Miss Newman. "It can be sixty miles wide and over ten thousand feet high."

WHAT?! I never heard of a haboob.

"Did you ever hear of a haboob?" I whispered to Andrea.

"No," she said. "That's a new one on me."

If the Human Dictionary never heard of a haboob, *nobody* did. Andrea knows everything.

I was beginning to think Miss Newman

might be crazy. She was just making stuff up.

"Some haboobs will travel a hundred miles," she continued. "The sand can be so thick, you can't see more than a few feet in front of you."

"That sounds scary," said Emily, who thinks everything is scary.

"Oh, don't worry," said Miss Newman. "Haboobs mostly hit dry desert regions, like the Sahara. They hardly ever hit this area."

I know what you're thinking. You're thinking that "haboob" might be a real word. You're thinking there's going to be a haboob later in this book.

Well, you're *wrong*! So nah-nah-nah boo-boo on you. No haboobs! From now on, this is a haboob-free book.

Don't bother looking "haboob" up in the dictionary. It's not there. Nothing exciting is going to happen for the rest of the book. No more lightning bolts. No haboobs. You might as well stop reading right now and pick up one of those Newbery books instead. Go ahead. You look like you could use a nap.

The *D* Word

"Pringle up, everybody!" said Mr. Cooper.

We walked a million hundred miles back to our classroom so we could work on reading, math, and other boring stuff. Then it was time for lunch, so we had to walk another million hundred miles to the vomitorium.

I sat with Ryan, Michael, Neil, and Alexia. Then, of course, Andrea and Emily came over and sat at our table.

I traded my peanut butter and jelly sandwich with Ryan. Ryan traded sandwiches with Michael. Michael traded sandwiches with Neil. Neil traded sandwiches with Alexia. Alexia traded sandwiches with Andrea. Andrea traded sandwiches with Emily. Emily traded sandwiches with me. So I got my peanut butter and jelly sandwich back.

"I'm worried about Luke Warm, that cue card guy," said Emily, who always worries about everything.

"I hope he doesn't get struck by lightning

again," said Ryan.

"Lightning never strikes twice in the same place," Michael said.

"That's because after lightning strikes once, the place isn't *there* anymore," I told them.

"Hey, I have an idea!" said Andrea. "We should make get well cards for Luke Warm! That will make him feel better!"

"Great idea, Andrea!" said Emily, who thinks all Andrea's ideas are great. "We can draw pictures for him."

If you ask me, those two *like* it when people get sick. It gives them an excuse to draw pictures of rainbows and butterflies and other girlie stuff.

Andrea and Emily took out their notebooks and started making get well cards for Luke Warm.

"Actually I'm more worried about Miss Newman," said Alexia.

"Why?" I asked.

"Well, she obviously doesn't know *anything* about the weather," Alexia replied. "She just reads Luke Warm's cue cards."

"Yeah, she's like a reading machine," said Neil.

Miss Newman isn't human!

"Hey," I said, "maybe Miss Newman isn't a *real* meteorologist after all. Did you ever think about that?"

"What do you mean, Arlo?" asked Andrea.

"Well, maybe she's just been *pretending* to be a meteorologist so she could be on TV. Maybe she kidnapped a *real* meteorologist and tied her to one of those weather blimps. Stuff like that happens all the time, y'know."

"I'm scared," said Emily, who's scared of everything.

"Yeah," added Michael. "The *real* meteorologist is probably dangling upside down from a rope below the blimp right now.

And it's floating away."

"To Antarctica," I added.

"We've got to *do* something!" shouted Emily. Then she went running out of the vomitorium.

Sheesh, get a grip! That girl will fall for *anything*.

"I don't like to say this," said Alexia, "but what if Miss Newman is . . ." She lowered her voice to a whisper. ". . . kind of dumb?"

"That's not a nice thing to say," said Andrea.

Andrea was right. "Dumb" is *not* a nice word. In fact, there's only one word in the English language that's worse than dumb.

"Dumbhead."

"We shouldn't call people dumb," said Neil. "Even if they *are* dumb."

"It wouldn't be Miss Newman's fault if she was dumb," said Alexia.

"Yeah, dumb people can't help it if they're dumb," I added.

"Can you all stop saying the *D* word?" asked Andrea. "It's not nice!"

"What will happen when Miss Newman gets back to Channel 4 to do the weather again?" asked Alexia. "Without Luke Warm's cue cards, she'll have nothing to say."

"She'll probably get fired," said Michael.

"That will be sad," said Alexia.

"Her whole *life* will be ruined," said Neil.

That made me wonder something. Do you think dumb people know they're dumb? Or are they too dumb to know how dumb they are?

I would think that if I was really dumb, I would never say anything to anybody, because I'd be afraid of saying something dumb. But I've noticed that dumb people seem to have no problems saying dumb things. So either they're so dumb that they don't know they're dumb, or they don't care that they're showing how dumb they are.

Hey, wait a minute. If dumb people are too dumb to know they're dumb, then maybe *I'm* dumb!

What if I'm so dumb that I don't know how dumb I am?

I think just to be on the safe side, I should just stop talking altogether. That's what a smart dumb person would do.

"Hey, I have an idea!" Ryan said. "We could teach Miss Newman about the weather! That way, when she goes back to Channel 4, she'll know what she's talking about and she won't get fired."*

"That's *genius*!" we all said.

Ryan should get the Nobel Prize for that idea.

---

*What are you looking down here for? The story's up there, dumbhead!

A Special Prize

It stopped raining, but the playground was still wet. So we had to have indoor recess. Ugh. I'm not sure which is worse, indoor recess or National Poetry Month.

"Can we go talk to Miss Newman?" Ryan asked Mr. Cooper when we got back to class. "We want to teach her about clouds and humidity and temperature and other weather stuff so she won't get fired."

"Miss Newman is talking with the fifth graders now," Mr. Cooper replied.

Bummer in the summer!

"Can we play board games?" asked Andrea.

"Sure!" said Mr. Cooper.

As it turned out, we didn't have to play boring board games after all. Because you'll never believe who walked through the door at that moment.

Nobody! You can't walk through a *door*. Doors are made of wood. But you'll never believe who walked through the door*way*.

It was Miss Newman!

"The children would like to talk to you about weather," Mr. Cooper told her.

"Oh, that stuff is *so* confusing," said Miss Newman. "How about we have a contest instead?"

"Oooh, I love contests!" said Andrea. "Do we get to win something?"

Andrea loves winning stuff. She probably has a room at home full of awards and trophies to show how good she is at everything. What is her problem? Why can't a truck full of trophies fall on her head?

"Of course!" said Miss Newman. "The winner will get a special prize."

"I love prizes!" shouted Andrea and Emily, clapping their hands together.

"How do we play?" asked Ryan.

"It's simple," said Miss Newman. "I'll ask some questions. Whoever gets the right answer to each question wins a point. At the end, the student with the most points wins the prize."

Hmmm. This was going to be weird. Miss Newman didn't seem to know anything without reading it off a cue card. How was she going to ask us questions?

"Ready?" she asked.

"Ready!"

"Okay, here's the first question," said Miss Newman. "Where do clouds go to the bathroom?"

"HUH?" we all said, which is also "HUH" backward.

That was a weird question. Clouds don't go to the bathroom.

Then it hit me. I knew the answer!

"Clouds go to the bathroom anywhere they want!" I shouted. "Because they're clouds!"

"Right!" said Miss Newman. "That's one point for A.J.!"

Yay! I got a point!

Andrea looked all mad. She hates it when she's not winning.

"Don't we have to raise our hands to answer the questions?" she asked.

"No," said Miss Newman. "The first person to shout out the correct answer wins the point. Next question. How is snow white?"

"HUH?" everybody said.

"How should I know how Snow White

is?" I shouted. "Ask the seven dwarfs!"

"Correct!" said Miss Newman. "That's two points for A.J.!"

"What?!" said Andrea. "That doesn't make any sense!"

Andrea was *really* mad now. I was afraid smoke might start pouring out of her ears.

Well, nah-nah-nah boo-boo on her. I was winning, 2–0.

"Next question," said Miss Neman. "Do you know why weather

wants its privacy?"

"HUH?"

I knew the answer to that one.

"Weather wants its privacy because it's always changing!" I shouted. "Get it?"

"That's right!" said Miss Newman. "Three points! You are *really* good at this game, A.J."

"Thank you!" I said, sticking my tongue out at Andrea. In her face!

"It's not fair!" Andrea shouted. "These questions are just silly!"

Andrea is such a sore loser. Now I had three points, and everybody else had nothing. This was the greatest day of my life.

"Let's move on to the next question," said Miss Newman. "Is it hard for gusts of wind to talk to each other?"

"HUH?"

I didn't know the answer to that one.

"No, it's a breeze!" shouted Andrea.

"Right!" said Miss Newman. "Andrea gets a point. Three-to-one."

Andrea stuck her tongue out at me.

"Next question," said Miss Newman. "Why don't meteorologists like going out to dinner on the moon?"

"HUH?"

I slapped my head. I didn't know that one either.

"Because there's no atmosphere!"

shouted Andrea.

"Correct!" said Miss Newman. "That's another point for Andrea. You're catching up. It's three-to-two now."

Andrea smiled the smile she smiles to let everybody know she knows something nobody else knows.

"Next question," said Miss Newman. "What does a meteorologist order in a Tex-Mex restaurant?"

"HUH?"

"Chili!" shouted Andrea.

"Yes!" said Miss Newman. "*Very* good, Andrea! Now it's all tied up at three-to-three. It's time for the tiebreaker. This will be the last question. If A.J. gets this one right, he will be the winner. If Andrea gets it right, *she* will be the winner."

Everybody was looking at me and Andrea. There was electricity in the air.

Well, not really. If there was electricity in the air, we would have all been electrocuted. But everybody was glued to their seats.

Well, not really. Why would anybody glue themselves to a seat? They'd get glue on their pants. Then they'd have to take the pants to a dry cleaner. But everybody was on pins and needles.

Well, not really. We were sitting on chairs. If we were on pins and needles, it would have hurt.

But it was *really* exciting! You should have *been* there! I *had* to beat Andrea.

"Okay, here's the last question," said Miss Newman. "What is the opposite of a hurricane?"

"HUH?"

The opposite of a hurricane? There's no opposite of a hurricane! "Up" is the opposite of "down." "Big" is the opposite of "little." But there's no opposite of a hurricane. The opposite of a hurricane would be *no* hurricane.

"No hurricane!" shouted Emily.

"Sorry, but that's wrong," said Miss Newman.

Hmmm. I looked at Ryan. Ryan looked

at Michael. Michael looked at Neil. Neil looked at Alexia. Alexia looked at me. Everybody was looking at each other. Nobody knew the answer.

I didn't know what to say. I didn't know what to do. I had to think fast. I was concentrating so hard that my brain hurt. I didn't want Andrea to win.

Then it hit me.

"The opposite of a hurricane," Andrea and I shouted at the exact same time, "is a himmicane!"

"That's *right*!" Miss Newman yelled. "You *both* get a point. A.J. and Andrea *both* win the prize!"

Everybody started yelling and

screaming and shrieking and hooting and hollering and freaking out.

"So what do we win?" asked Andrea.

"You win . . . ," said Miss Newman, ". . . a ride in the Channel 4 weather balloon!"

Numbers

WHAT?!

I thought the prize was going to be a candy bar, or a million dollars. I didn't want to go on a balloon ride with Andrea.

"Ooooo!" Ryan said. "A.J. and Andrea are going on a balloon ride together. They must be in *love!*"

"When are you gonna get married?" asked Michael.

If those guys weren't my best friends, I would hate them.

"Ryan, you can go on the balloon ride instead of me," I said.

"Really?" Ryan replied. "Cool!"

"I'm sorry, boys," said Miss Newman, "but A.J. won the contest fair and square. He can't give the prize away."

"Uh . . . I have to go to the bathroom," I said. "Maybe I'll go on the balloon ride some other time."

"You do *not* have to go to the bathroom, Arlo!" Andrea said. "You're just saying that because you don't want to go on the balloon ride with me."

Andrea put her hands on her hips. And you know what it means when girls put their hands on their hips.*

There was no way out of it. I had to go on the balloon ride with Andrea. Ugh.

"Okay, everybody!" shouted Mr. Cooper. "Pringle up!"

We walked to the playground. Mr. Klutz was out there next to the Channel 4 weather balloon, tied to the ground with ropes.

Well, the *balloon* was tied to the ground with ropes, not Mr. Klutz. It would be weird if Mr. Klutz was tied to the ground with ropes.

---

*It means they're mad. Nobody knows why.

"Do I *have* to go on the balloon ride?" I asked.

"This is going to be *fun*, A.J.!" he told me. "It's a once-in-a-lifetime experience!"

Having an elephant fall on your head would be a once-in-a-lifetime experience too, but I don't want *that* to happen.

Miss Newman climbed into the basket under the balloon. Andrea climbed into the basket next. Then I climbed in. The basket was small. There was just enough room in there for the three of us and a video camera.

"Bon voyage!" shouted Mr. Klutz.

Huh? He was suddenly talking French for no reason!

"Ten . . . nine . . . eight . . . ," everybody

started chanting, "seven . . . six . . . five . . ."

I held on to the side of the basket.

". . . four . . . three . . . two . . . one . . ."

"Okay, release the ropes!" yelled Miss Newman.

"Bye!" all the kids shouted.

The balloon started rising. It felt like I was in an elevator, but there were no buttons. The ground fell away.

"Wheeee!" shouted Andrea. "This is *fun*!"

Not for me. I thought I was gonna die.

"Is something wrong, A.J.?" asked Miss Newman.

"No, nothing," I replied.

"You're pale as a ghost," she said, putting her hand on my forehead.

"I'm fine."

"You're sweating, Arlo," Andrea said. "You look sick. What is it?"

I closed my eyes.

"Okay," I finally admitted. "I'm afraid of heights."

There, I said it. It's *scary* being in high places. I don't like to be in an airplane. I don't like to be in tall buildings. I don't even like elevators. We were rising higher and higher over the roof of the school.

"Let's go back down," Andrea said. "Arlo looks like he's going to pass out."

"It's too late to go back down now," said Miss Newman. "Why didn't you tell me earlier that you were afraid of heights,

A.J.? I would have picked somebody else to take the balloon ride."

"I didn't want my friends to know," I said.

"It's nothing to be ashamed of, Arlo," Andrea told me. "*Lots* of people are afraid of heights. I looked it up on my smartphone. It's called acrophobia."

Andrea looks *everything* up so she can prove how smart she is.

"Promise me you won't tell anybody," I said. "If the guys find out I have acrophobia, they'll make fun of me for the rest of my life."

"Okay," Andrea said. "Hold on, Arlo."

"We'll get you through this, A.J.," said Miss Newman.

We waved to everybody down on the playground. I tried to smile, but it felt like my stomach was going to fall out of my body. This was the worst day of my life. I wanted to go to Antarctica and live with the penguins.

"Isn't it beautiful?" asked Andrea.

I didn't know if it was beautiful or not.

I had my eyes closed. But that just made it worse. Andrea and Miss Newman were holding on to me. I opened my eyes again. We were floating above the trees. The school looked really small. We were getting higher and higher.

"I don't feel good," I said.

"Are you going to be okay, A.J.?" asked Miss Newman.

"I have to go to the bathroom," I said.

"Balloons don't have bathrooms, Arlo!" Andrea said.

"Well, I have to go. I told you that before."

"I thought you just said that to get out of riding in the balloon with me," replied Andrea.

"No, I had to go to the bathroom!" I told

her. "I still do. Can't I just climb up on the edge here and—"

"Noooooo!" shouted Andrea and Miss Newman.

"Do you have to go number one or number two?" asked Andrea.

"Number three."

"Number three?" she said. "What's number three? I never heard of number three."

"I'm not sure I *want* to know what number three is," said Miss Newman.

"I thought you were so good in math," I told Andrea. "Number three is when you have to do a number one and a number two at the same time. Two plus one equals three."

"Okay, that's too much information," said Miss Newman.

"And it's gross," added Andrea.

"What's *really* gross is number *four*," I told them.

"Number *four*?" both of them said.

"What's *that*?" Andrea asked me. "I never heard of number four."

Ha! Finally, I knew something Andrea didn't know.

"Believe me," I told her. "You don't *want* to know what number four is."

"Try to hold it in, Arlo," Andrea told me. "We'll be back on the ground soon. Right, Miss Newman?"

Miss Newman didn't answer. She was looking at me.

"What *is* number four?" she asked.

"Do you really want to know?"

"Yes!" both of them replied.

"Okay, number four is when—"

I didn't have the chance to finish my

sentence, because at that moment the weirdest thing in the history of the world happened. A blast of water hit us in the face!

"We're heading into a storm!" shouted Miss Newman.

She was right. The sky was suddenly dark all around us, and the rain was coming down hard.

"It's raining cats and dogs!" Andrea shouted.

That was a total lie. I didn't see any animals falling out of the sky. It was just rain. We were already soaked. It was coming down so hard that it was blowing *sideways*. The basket was swaying back and forth. I was afraid we might fall out!

"This looks like a Category 1 or a Category 2 storm," shouted Miss Newman. "It could even be Category 3."

"Is a Category 3 storm a Category 1 storm and a Category 2 storm put together?" I asked.

"It's not like going to the bathroom, Arlo!" shouted Andrea.

"I'm afraid this might be a Category 4 storm!" shouted Miss Newman.

Uh-oh. That can't be good.

There was another blast of wind, and then suddenly the rain stopped and I was hit in the face with sand or dust or dirt or something. I closed my eyes just in time.

"What's going on?" shouted Andrea. "Are we in the middle of a hurricane?"

"No," Miss Newman shouted back.

"Is it a himmicane?" I asked.

"No," shouted Miss Newman. "It's a haboob!"

Okay, So I Lied

Okay, so I lied.* I told you there was no such thing as a haboob, and there would be no more haboobs in this book. And guess what? It turns out "haboob" is a real word, and it's part of the story!

---

*I'm really sorry about that. Lying is not a nice thing. But if I told you back in Chapter Five that there was going to be a haboob in Chapter Eight, it wouldn't have been a big surprise when the haboob hit. Aren't surprises fun?

"Cover your faces!" yelled Miss New-man. "Keep the sand out of your eyes and nose!"

She didn't have to tell me. I pulled my T-shirt over my face to keep the sand away.

"What are we going to do?" shouted Andrea.

"There's nothing to do but ride it out!" Miss Newman yelled back. "The haboob could be moving forty miles an hour."

Wow! That might be fast enough to blow the school away. And if the school blows away, there will be no school! Yay!

But right now I had other things to worry about. The basket was swaying back and forth. I was afraid the whole thing might flip over.

"Are we going to die?" I shouted.

"Not on *my* watch," Miss Newman shouted back.

What did watches have to do with anything? She wasn't even wearing a watch.

Miss Newman grabbed some ropes on the side of the basket and pulled on them. I guess it was for steering or something. The basket stopped swaying.

"This is a dangerous situation," she hollered over the sound of the wind and sand blowing in our faces. "I need to report the weather to the people!"

"How are you going to do that?" Andrea shouted.

"Grab that camera off the floor," Miss Newman yelled. "We have a satellite linkup so we can transmit the signal back to Channel 4."

"I have sand in my eyes!" Andrea hollered. "I can't see!"

"I got it," I yelled as I picked up the camera. "What do you want me to do?"

"Push the red button and point the camera at me," Miss Newman yelled back.

I did what she said.

"This is Sprinkles Newman, of Channel 4 weather," she hollered. "I'm coming to you live from the middle of a haboob. That's an intense sandstorm. If you're outside, I need you to get inside right away. If you can't get inside, cover your nose and mouth with cloth."

The camera was heavy. But I kept

pointing it at Miss Newman.

"If you're in your car driving some-where, pull over right away," she shouted. "Almost every death caused by a haboob has been because people try to drive cars through them and they crash into things."

She went on like that for a while, talk-ing about which direction the haboob was heading and how fast it was moving. She sure knows a lot about haboobs!

Finally, the haboob blew past us. The sky got calm. Miss Newman steered the balloon so we were coming down in a field across the street from where we took off. The whole school came running over.

Well, not really. Schools can't run.

They don't have legs. But all the kids and teachers came running over. They were cheering and clapping.

"We saw you on TV!" everybody shouted.

"That was cool, A.J.," said Neil. "You're famous!"

This was the greatest day of my life. Mr. Klutz helped us climb out of the basket. All the teachers were taking pictures with their cell phones.

"Arlo, you were *sooooo* brave filming that video!" said Andrea.

And then she did the most horrible thing in the history of the world. She kissed me!

Ugh, gross! This was the worst day of my life!

"Ooooo!" Ryan said. "Andrea kissed A.J. and said he was brave. They must be in *love*!"

"When are you gonna get married?" asked Michael.

The *L* Word

When we got back to school, it was time for dismissal. We pringled up near the front door by the office. All the parents must have been worried about their kids getting caught in the haboob. I could see a bunch of them through the front door.

And you'll never believe who came

running through the front door at that moment.

Nobody! You can't run through the front door! It's made of glass. You'd just smash your head into it. But you'll never believe who opened the front door and came running into the school.

It was Luke Warm! I thought he was going to be in the hospital for a long time after getting struck by lightning. But he looked okay. He was holding a stack of his cards.

Miss Newman ran over to him.

"Luke!" she shouted, putting her arms around him. Then she kissed him. Ugh, gross!

"Is she giving him mouth-to-mouth resuscitation again?" Ryan asked.

"No, dumbhead," said Andrea. "She's kissing him!"

If you ask me, kissing looks way too much like mouth-to-mouth resuscitation.

"Ooooo!" Ryan said. "Miss Newman is kissing Luke Warm. They must be in *love!*"

"When are you gonna get married?" asked Michael.

Luke Warm held up one of his cards for Miss Newman to read. It said: I CAN'T HEAR OR SPEAK BECAUSE OF THE

LIGHTNING. I SHOULD BE FINE IN A FEW WEEKS.

Miss Newman took one of Luke's cards and wrote this on it: I MISSED YOU!

Luke Warm held up another card: I MISSED YOU TOO!

Miss Newman took another card and wrote this on it: I'M SO GLAD YOU'RE BACK!

Luke Warm held up another card: ME TOO!

Miss Newman took another card and wrote this on it: I DON'T KNOW WHAT I WOULD DO WITHOUT YOU!

Luke Warm held up another card: THE SAME GOES FOR ME!

Hey, this was getting *way* too mushy.

Miss Newman took another card and wrote this on it: I LOVE YOU, LUKE!

Luke Warm held up another card: I LOVE YOU, SPRINKLES!

Ugh, gross! They used the *L* word!

Then Luke Warm and Miss Newman started kissing again. I thought I was gonna die.

Man, there sure is a lot of kissing in this book.

"That's the most romantic thing I've ever seen," Andrea said. "I think I'm going to cry!"

Then Luke Warm and Miss Newman both picked up cards and started writing on them.

They held them up.

Both of the cards said the same thing: WILL YOU MARRY ME?*

---

*I can't believe you're still reading this. Really, you should close this book. I told you once already. Don't you have anything better to do with your life? There's a whole world out there. TV shows to watch. Video games to play. Stop wasting your life on dumb books like this!

11

Pigs in Blankets

The next day Miss Newman was back on Channel 4 doing the weather again. It looked like she really knew what she was talking about. But we all knew that behind the camera Luke Warm was holding up cards for her to read.

The next weekend the whole school was invited to the wedding.

Well, not really. Just the teachers and students were invited. Schools don't go to weddings.

It was held in a big field next to the Channel 4 weather balloon. They had musicians playing weird songs like "Stormy Weather," "Baby, It's Cold Outside," and "Raindrops Keep Falling on My Head."

We had to wait a million hundred hours for the ceremony to begin. Finally the minister stood up and everybody got quiet.

"We are gathered here together," he said, "to blah blah blah this man and this woman blah blah blah holy matrimony blah blah blah."

It went on like that for a while.

"Do you promise to love and honor each other," the minister said, "in rain and in sunshine, in high and low humidity, during heat warnings and cold fronts, in droughts and in thunderstorms, regardless of the wind chill factor?"

Miss Newman held up a card. It said: I DO.

Luke Warm held up a card. It said: I DO.

"I now pronounce you husband and wife," said the minister.

What happened next was totally gross.

"Is he giving her mouth-to-mouth resuscitation again?" I asked.

"No!" said Andrea. "They're kissing!"

"Oooooo!" Ryan said. "Miss Newman is kissing Luke Warm! They must be in *love*!"

"When are they gonna get married?" asked Michael.

"They just *did*, you dumbheads!" shouted Andrea.

When the wedding was over, there was a big party. We got to eat little hot dogs. They're called pigs in blankets. Nobody knows why. If you put a *real* pig in a blanket, it wouldn't be called a hot dog. And it would be gross.

Anyway, I was eating my hundred millionth pig in a blanket when Andrea came over to me.

"Wasn't the wedding romantic, Arlo?" she asked.

"No."

"Maybe someday *we'll* get married, Arlo," Andrea said.

"Only if I get hit by lightning and my brain doesn't work anymore," I told her.

After the party, Miss Newman and Luke Warm climbed into the basket under the weather balloon. They were leaving for their honeymoon at the headquarters of the National Weather Service.

"Ten ... nine ... eight ... seven ... six ... five ... four ... three ... two ... one ..."

"Release the ropes!"

Everybody was waving and saying stuff in French as the balloon went up in the air. Miss Newman and Luke Warm held up a card and showed it to us before they floated away. It said: GOOD-BYE!

Well, that's pretty much what happened. Maybe Miss Newman will learn about the weather so she won't have to rely on cue cards all the time. Maybe the *real* meteorologist will escape from the weather blimp she's dangling from upside down. Maybe Mr. Klutz will get his eyes checked and stop talking in French for no reason. Maybe deer will get head lice. Maybe grown-ups will stop giving each other mouth-to-mouth resuscitation just for the fun of it. Maybe dumb people will realize how dumb they are and stop saying dumb things. Maybe the seven dwarfs will let us know how Snow White is. Maybe meteorologists will go out for dinner on the moon. Maybe people will stop putting glue on their pants. Maybe animals will fall out of the sky. Maybe someday I'll tell you what number four is. Maybe you'll return this book to the bookstore and get your money back.

But it won't be easy!